For Noun, my everyday cat
Catharina

BRUNO

SOME OF THE MORE INTERESTING DAYS IN MY LIFE SO FAR

Story by Catharina Valckx
Illustrations by Nicolas Hubesch

Translated by Antony Shugaar

GECKO PRESS

A peculiar day

The peculiar day started out as an ordinary day.
I was walking down the street, and it was a little windy, but not very.
Not a gale, just a light breeze.

All of a sudden, a fish appeared, right beside me.
She was swimming through the air.

"Hello," I said. "Shouldn't you be in the water?"
"Yes," the fish replied. "I can't understand it.
Something very strange is going on..."

The fish followed me. Perhaps because I'd spoken to her.
She felt a little lost, I think.
I went into Gloria's shop to buy milk.
The fish was still with me, so she came inside.

"Hello, Bruno!" Gloria called out, as usual.
Then she saw the fish and her eyes went wide.
The fish was very shy. Gloria asked her if she liked milk.

She replied in a very small voice that she'd never tried any.
Of course she hadn't! This was the first time she'd been out of the water!
Gloria insisted she try some of her milk, and the fish didn't dare refuse.

Outcome: the fish felt sick.
"It's very odd that my milk made her ill," said Gloria.

"Not at all," I replied. "Fish don't drink milk.
They drink water with specks of seaweed in it."
"Mhm," the fish confirmed, in such a small voice we could barely hear her.

Just then, Ringo, the old pony, came in.
Backwards. He said hello and added: "It's very peculiar,
I only seem to be able to walk like this today. Backwards!"

In spite of his problem, Ringo really wanted a glass of milk.
So did I, for that matter. But all at once the fish began
to make little gasps. She didn't look at all well.
"Quick, she has to go back in the water," I said.

Gloria stayed behind in her shop.
That was normal; there was no one to take her
place. Even on the most peculiar days,
certain things remain normal, I've noticed.
Ringo, the fish, and I hurried to the riverbank.
The fish was trembling all over, poor little thing.

I was about to throw her into the water,
when she said in a very low voice, "Follow me."
"What do you mean, Follow me?" I asked.
"Follow me into the water."

"But…I'm a cat," I said.
Oddly enough, though, I wanted to follow her.
Ringo too. He said, "Why not, since we're here!"

What was peculiar was that we could breathe underwater
no problem, and without swallowing any. It was fantastic.

Right away, the fish felt much better.
She told us that her name was Bup. Which isn't an
odd name for a fish, apparently. There are plenty called that.
Bup introduced us to her family and friends.

Underwater, old Ringo felt twenty years younger.
He began to swim backwards at top speed.
That made all the little fish laugh.
So we all had a backwards swimming race with Ringo.

And it was our friend Bup who won! It's a little
peculiar that Bup won the race since she'd been feeling
so unwell just a short while ago. But that's okay.
On peculiar days, nothing should come as a surprise.

Night fell suddenly. As if someone had switched off
the lights. I couldn't see a thing. Just a scrap of slightly
phosphorescent seaweed. I felt around for Ringo.
Then we kissed Bup goodbye
(at least, I hope that was Bup) and we left.

Ringo walked home with me. No longer backwards.
Everything had returned to normal.
I told him, "That was the most peculiar day of my life."
And Ringo made me laugh when he replied:
"I'd be glad to have a peculiar day like that one every day of my life!"
I didn't say anything, but if every day was peculiar,
then they wouldn't be peculiar anymore, would they? Ha, ha!

Sometimes I can be very intelligent,
even when I'm completely wet and tired out.

A rainy day

That morning, when I looked out the window, I saw a curtain of rain.
The rain was falling so hard it hid everything else.

Oh well, I said to myself, there's no hurry to go anywhere this morning…
I was just going to have my breakfast when someone knocked at the door.

It was Ringo. He was soaked like a sponge.
"What are you doing outside in weather like this?" I asked.

"My house is no better inside than out," said Ringo. "It's leaking everywhere."
"Come on in," I said.

Ringo was gulping down my hot milk when, again, someone
knocked at my door. It was Georgette, the turtledove.
She too was as soaked as a sponge.

"It's impossible to fly in this weather," said Georgette.
"And if I walk, I'll drown in the puddles."
"Come on in," I said.

Ringo and Georgette were joyfully sampling my jams
when, once again, someone knocked at the door.
"Don't open it, Bruno," Ringo said, "there's not much jam left."

"He's right," Georgette confirmed, "there's just enough for the three of us."
Unbelievable, isn't it? Those two were so selfish!
Of course I went to open the door.

But I shouldn't have. It was the dreaded Gerard. As soaked as a sponge.
He shoved me aside and rushed into the kitchen.

"I saw a nice plump turtledove come in here,"
dreadful Gerard growled, shaking his fur coat.

"Really?" Ringo stammered. "A turtledove?
I'm pretty sure she left."
"I didn't see her leave," growled the dreaded Gerard.
"That's because you can't see a thing in this rain," I said.

Dreadful Gerard sniffed the air.
"She's still here. My nose never fails me. I can smell a turtledove in here."
He started searching everywhere. In the cupboards, in the fridge, even in the oven.
Hiding under the table, Georgette was scared to death.

Just then, in the broom cupboard, the dreaded Gerard found my umbrella.
"An umbrella!" he cried, as if he'd found the treasure of the forty thieves.
He opened it, examined it, and then his mouth opened
in a huge smile that showed all his teeth.

Dreadful Gerard was so happy with his find that he forgot all about Georgette!
He went back out into the rain without even saying goodbye.
I'd lost my umbrella, but we were curiously relieved, I can tell you.
Especially Georgette.

It went on pouring all afternoon.
Ringo and Georgette were glad to be warm and dry.
"And above all, I'm glad to be alive!" said Georgette.
It's just a shame you've run out of jam, Bruno."

Goodness me, I said to myself. I'm very fond of Ringo and Georgette,
but as soon as the rains stops, they're out the door!

A day when the power went out

That day, the power went out on my street.
At night, so as not to be in the dark, I lit candles. It was very pretty.

Since they don't happen very often,
I really like days when the power goes out.

A stupid day
(that ends pretty well)

That day was a stupid day. But I didn't know that yet. It was sunny, and I was meeting my friend Ringo, the old pony, for a picnic in the park.

I rang Ringo's doorbell. From the window
high above, he shouted down, "Come on up, Bruno!
I can't come down, I've sprained my ankle!"

So things were off to a flying start! I went upstairs. Guess what Ringo had done.
He was skipping down the stairs with his eyes shut.
Talk about stupid. With his eyes shut! At his age!

"Too bad about the fine weather," I said.
"We'll have to have our picnic indoors."
I hadn't prepared all that food for nothing.
I spread the picnic blanket out on the bed.

A crow landed on the windowsill and started to chatter.
"It's unhygienic to eat on a bed. What's more, that blanket…
it's a disgusting canary yellow, *cark*! I hate canaries."

It's no fun listening to a completely stupid crow.
Especially during a picnic that's already pretty bad.
"Why, do you know any canaries personally?" Ringo asked him.
"No, I don't! But there's been one at Gloria's shop
since this morning. A lost canary."

I happen to like yellow and I happen to like canaries.
I decided to go straight over to Gloria's to buy some milk,
and especially to take a look at this little lost canary.

While I was crossing the street, I came very close
to being run over by a family of wild boars.
On stupid days, you have to pay attention, that's for sure.

At Gloria's, I saw the canary right away. He was all crestfallen.
"He just flew up there," Gloria told me. "I don't know where he comes from.
And he doesn't seem to know either. Do you, Tweety?"
"His name is Tweety?" I asked.

"I decided to call him that," Gloria said.
"He talks, but you can't follow a thing he says. He mixes up his words."
"Caramel for the bridges," Tweety said.
"You see? He talks nonsense."
"Would you like to come on a picnic, Tweety?" I asked.
"Motorcoach," Tweety replied, with a faint smile.
I understood that to mean something along the lines of yes.

Out in the street, Tweety took to the air.
I thought he was going to fly away.

But no.
He made three small circles,
then landed on my head.
"PJs!" he chirped in delight.
I don't know exactly what he
meant by "PJs" but, in any case,
he stayed with me.

I went back to Ringo's place with Tweety.
"Ringo, let me introduce you to Tweety. Tweety, Ringo."
"Caw! How ugly that rotten canary is!"
squawked the stupid crow, who was still there.

"Salad drum!" Tweety shot back.
That made me laugh, but it was clear that
Tweety was upset. His eyes were full of tears.

I went right up close to that oaf of a crow and
roared like a ferocious lion. Grooaarr!
It got the fright of its life and flew away.
Ha ha! Good riddance.

But what's awful is that my ferocious roar scared Tweety too.
He also flew away. Ringo and I stood unhappily at the window,
hoping he'd come back. But he didn't.

I didn't feel much like staying at Ringo's.
That glutton had already eaten practically everything anyway.
And after all that, I'd forgotten to buy milk.
It really was the most pointless picnic of my life.

I came close to being run over again by the same wild boars.
Unbelievable, isn't it? Were they doing it on purpose or what?

I went to the park. I tried to console myself with the thought
that at least with a stupid day you're happy when it's over.
Much happier than you are at the end of a really nice day.
I was about to fall asleep when I heard a small joyous voice:
"Chic, chic, electric!"

It was Tweety! I was very happy to see him again.
And since there were still a few crumbs at the bottom of the basket,
we had a mini-picnic, just Tweety and me. Feasting on next to nothing.

You might say that, for a stupid day, this one ended perfectly.
True enough. And as Tweety would say: "Oodles of doodles!"

A much less interesting day

An almost perfect day

That morning, as I watched clouds go by,
I thought of how days go by, like clouds, each one different.
Good days, bad days, so-so days…
And I wondered what a perfect day would be like.

I thought it over and made a list of everything I'd want to do on a perfect day:

1. See Tweety, the canary.
2. See Ringo, the old pony.
3. Play with them (Tweety and Ringo).
4. Find treasure and give it to a poor starving family.
    (Now that's a great idea, if you ask me. Very heroic.)
5. Have ice cream with my friends, and maybe even
    with the poor starving animals.

All right then, I said to myself. If I can do all that in one day, it will be perfect.
I'm starting right now.

I went to see Tweety, number one on my list.
Tweety had found a place to live nearby.

I asked him if he wanted to come over to Ringo's.

"Steam train to paradise!" replied Tweety,
who always scrambles his words, and he fluttered after me.

When we got to Ringo's, Georgette was there too. She wasn't on my list. Still, things were going really well! This was turning out to be a very nice day. I'd reached number three on my list: playing with my friends.

We came up with the idea of all going together to the station. But not to catch a train...

...to play on the big escalators!
Ringo, Tweety, Georgette, and I all love
riding up and down the escalators.

Tweety was irrepressible, chirping the whole time:
"Hello I'm listening! Surprise party!"
The animals all wondered who was this little scatterbrain.

As I rode up for the twenty-eighth time,
I noticed a parcel lying at the top of the escalator.
Ah! I said to myself, this might be the treasure!

I carefully unwrapped
the parcel. It was a
nice crate of carrots.
"Yum, said Ringo.
"Don't touch them!" I said.
"I have a plan. I'm going to
give them to poor
starving animals."

I know where a family of poor rabbits live.
But just as we left the station, a big raccoon
came rushing after me shouting:
"Stop, thief! Stop, thief!"

"I'm not a thief!" I told him.
"I found these carrots and I'm going to give them to the poor."
"Sure you are!" shouted the raccoon. "And your stepmother's the
Queen of England! Give me my carrots or I'll call the police!"

He was going to bite me, that rabid beast!
I put down the crate and walked away.

So much for helping the poor. I didn't become a hero after all.
At least, not that day. But I'd done my best, and that's not bad.
(Ringo told me that to cheer me up.)

Georgette suggested we go and get ice cream.
The last item on my list! It's not as easy as it seems to have
a perfect day, but good ice cream helps a lot. Yum.

On my way home, while crossing the bridge, I saw Bup.
Dear little Bup, I'd forgotten to put her on my list!
I called out, "Hey! Bup! It's me!"
Bup jumped out of the water and called back, "Hi there, Bruno!"
then plop, she fell back in. She jumped out again and asked,
"You doing all right?" and then plop, she fell back in.

"Yes!" I answered. "I'm doing fine! Today was an almost perfect day!" and plop, my cap fell into the water. I watched it drift downstream.

My cap was lost.
Suddenly it wasn't a perfect day at all.
It was an almost ruined day.

This edition first published in 2017 by Gecko Press
PO Box 9335, Marion Square, Wellington 6141, New Zealand
info@geckopress.com

English language edition © Gecko Press Ltd 2017
Translation © Antony Shugaar 2017

Original title: *Bruno. Quelques jours de ma vie très intéressante*
Text by Catharina Valckx, illustrations by Nicolas Hubesch
© 2015 l'école des loisirs, Paris

Distributed in the United States and Canada by
Lerner Publishing Group, www.lernerbooks.com
Distributed in the United Kingdom by
Bounce Sales and Marketing, www.bouncemarketing.co.uk
Distributed in Australia by Scholastic Australia, www.scholastic.com.au
Distributed in New Zealand by Upstart Distribution, www.upstartpress.co.nz

Edited by Penelope Todd
Cover design by Vida & Luke Kelly
Book design and typesetting by Katrina Duncan
Printed in China by Everbest Printing Co Ltd,
an accredited ISO 14001 & FSC certified printer

ISBN hardback: 978-1-77657-124-6
ISBN paperback: 978-1-77657-125-3

For more curiously good books, visit www.geckopress.com